D0120262

This book belongs to:

.....

.....

Retold by Sue Graves
Illustrated by Adrienne Salgado

Reading consultants: Betty Root and Monica Hughes

Marks and Spencer p.l.c.
PO Box 3339
Chester, CH99 9QS

shop online
www.marksandspencer.com

Copyright © Exclusive Editions 2006

First Readers is a trade mark of Exclusive Editions Limited.

All rights reserved. No part of this publication may be reproduced, stored in a retrieval system, or transmitted in any form or by any means, electronic, mechanical, photocopying, recording or otherwise, without the prior permission of the copyright owner.

ISBN 978-1-84461-582-7
Printed in China

The Elves and the Shoemaker

MARKS &
SPENCER

Helping your child to read

First Readers are closely linked to the National Curriculum. Their vocabulary has been carefully selected from the word lists recommended by the National Literacy Strategy.

Read the story

Read the story to your child a few times.

When it was time for bed, the shoemaker hid.
Soon, the two elves came out to play.
They saw the leather.
They saw the shoes and boots cut ou
The elves sewed the shoes.
Then they sewed the boots.
They sewed them very neatly.
"What kind elves," the shoemaker
to himself.

20

Follow your finger

Run your finger under the text as you read. Your child will soon begin to follow the words with you.

Look at the pictures

Talk about the pictures. They will help your child to understand the story.

Have a go

Let your child have a go at reading the large type on each right-hand page. It repeats a line from the story.

Join in

When your child is ready, encourage them to join in with the main story text. Shared reading is the first step to reading alone.

Once, a shoemaker and his wife
lived in a shoe shop.
They were very poor.
One day, the shoemaker had only
one piece of leather left.
It was very small.
The shoemaker cut out some shoes and
went to bed.

The shoemaker cut out some shoes.

That night, two elves came out to play.
They saw the leather.
They saw the shoes cut out.
So the elves sewed the shoes.
They sewed them very neatly.

The elves sewed the shoes.

The next morning, the shoemaker found the shoes.
"What lovely shoes!" he said.
Just then, a woman came into the shoe shop.
She tried on the shoes.
"These shoes are just right," she said.
She gave the shoemaker some money.

"These shoes are just right."

The shoemaker bought a big
piece of leather.
He cut out some boots and went
to bed.
That night, the two elves came out to
play again.
They saw the leather.
They saw the boots cut out.
So the elves sewed the boots.
They sewed them very neatly.

The elves sewed the boots.

The next morning the shoemaker found the boots.
"What lovely boots!" he said.
Just then, a man came into the shoe shop.
He took off his shoes and tried on the boots.
"These boots are just right," he said.
He gave the shoemaker some money.

"These boots are just right."

The shoemaker bought a bigger piece of leather.
He cut out some shoes and some boots.
"Who is making the shoes and boots?" said the shoemaker's wife.
"I will find out!" said the shoemaker.
"I will hide and see who comes to make them for me."

"Who is making the shoes and boots?"

When it was time for bed, the shoemaker hid.
Soon, the two elves came out to play.
They saw the leather.
They saw the shoes and boots cut out.
The elves sewed the shoes.
Then they sewed the boots.
They sewed them very neatly.
"What kind elves," the shoemaker said to himself.

The shoemaker hid.

The shoemaker told his wife about the elves.
"How can we thank them?" he said.
"Let's make shoes for them!" said the shoemaker's wife.
The shoemaker got his finest piece of leather.
Then they made some tiny shoes.

They made some tiny shoes.

Then the shoemaker and his wife hid.
Soon, the elves came out to play.
They tried on the tiny shoes.
The tiny shoes were perfect.

The tiny shoes were perfect.

After that, lots of people came to buy the shoes and boots at the shoe shop. And the shoemaker and his wife were never poor again.

They were never poor again.

Look back in your book.
Can you read these words?

shoemaker

shoes

wife

elves

boots

shoe shop

Can you answer these questions?

Who bought some shoes?

Who bought some boots?

Who made the shoes for the shoemaker?

First Readers

(subject to availability)

Beauty and the Beast
Cinderella
The Elves and the Shoemaker
The Emperor's New Clothes
The Enormous Turnip
The Gingerbread Man
Goldilocks and the Three Bears
Hansel and Gretel
Jack and the Beanstalk
Little Red Riding Hood
The Princess and the Pea
Rapunzel
Rumpelstiltskin
Sleeping Beauty
Snow White and the Seven Dwarfs
The Three Billy Goats Gruff
The Three Little Pigs
The Ugly Duckling